What Color Is Your Tooth Fairy?

Written by Whispering Dreams

Illustrated by Matthew Benton

LUMINARE PRESS

EUGENE, OREGON

Printed in the United States of America

Illustrations: Matthew Benton

Luminare Press
467 W 17th Ave
Eugene, OR 97401
www.luminarepress.com

ISBN: 978-1-937303-42-6

To Team Tooth Fairy:

Michael, Mike, Miquel, Gabby, Cruz, Emma,

Addie, Ty, Shelly, Dave, Linda, Jennifer

With Love and Gratitude

To Paxton,
All my love,
The Grand
Tooth Fairy

Gather 'round children,

Because this is known to very few,

It's the story of the Tooth Fairies

And the teeth they collect from you.

In the Pacific Ocean with waters of bluest blue,

There lies a string of islands connected by Tooth Lagoon.

In these Pacific Islands
On the biggest of all,
You'll see a splendid flow of water
Called Tooth Fairy Falls.

Looking past the falling water

Lies a scene you won't believe,

Of beautiful magical fairies

In the glow of a rainbow's gleam.

But most of all you'll notice the brilliant color of their wings.

They shimmer and they shine blue, pink, red, orange, and green.

It all started one day when Grandmother Rose found a book.

A razzle dazzle of rainbows and colors, one look was all it took.

The book was full of wonder and things she had never seen.

The razzle keeps you young, the dazzle gives you wings.

She read the magical book
For all the fairies to hear,
With a wisp and a whoosh
The tooth wand appeared.

Her wand was something special,
A truly wondrous sight.
Grandmother Rose transformed,
Into the Grand Tooth Fairy that night.

The other fairies took notice,

And began their lifelong dream.

For when a child loses their very first tooth,

A fairy gets their wings.

The Dazzling Ceremony takes place
At Tooth Fairy Falls,
That very magical day
When fairy destiny calls.
With a wisp of her wand
Through the rainbow above,
The Grand Tooth Fairy assigns
Her color with love.

The new Tooth Fairy

Twirls through the air with delight,

Now is the time

To take her first flight.

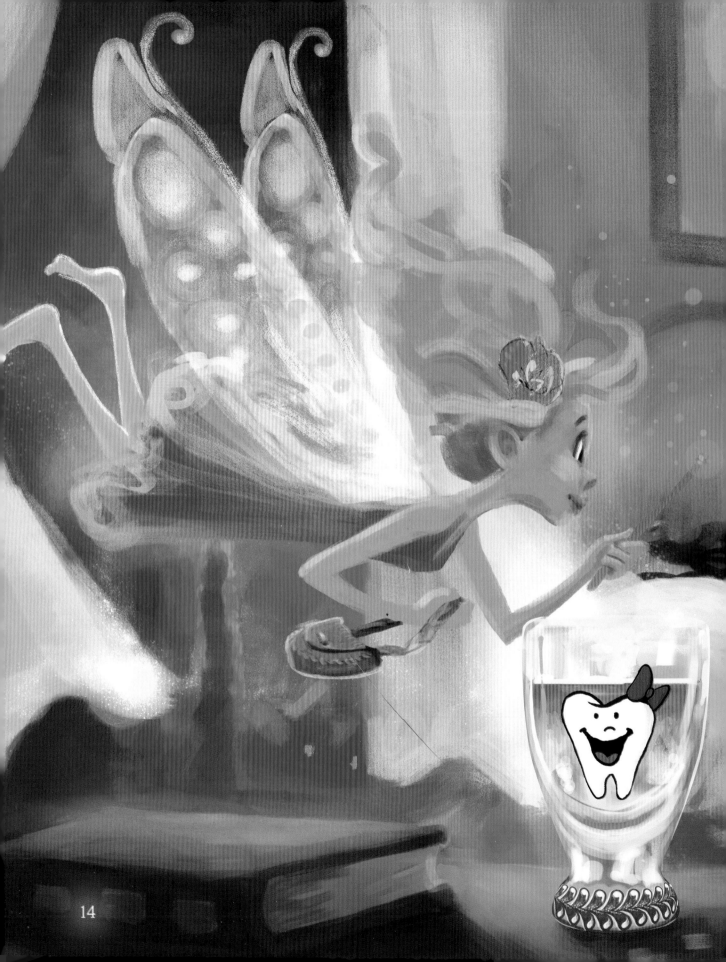

14

With a wand in her hand
And a satchel by her side,
She flies into the room
The starry night as her guide.

She gathers the tooth

From the glass meant for her.

What color is your Tooth Fairy?

In the morning you'll know for sure.

Her work is now done
The fairy flies away.
Back to Fairy Falls she goes
To await another day.

Don't forget to put your tooth in the glass
And fill with water all the way.
Your Tooth Fairy's color will be revealed
In the light of a new day.

Whispering Dreams was created by Nikki Castillo and Jessie Nolop. Nikki is an experienced glass painter and Jessie has a background in business and sales. These two moms shared a desire to create a product and tradition centered around the Tooth Fairy to enhance children's imaginations.

THE TOOTH FAIRY GLASS

A TOOTH FAIRY TRADITION

www.thetoothfairyglass.com